WELCOME TO

Beast Quest

Collect the special coins in this book.
You will earn one gold coin for
every chapter you read.

Once you have finished all the chapters,
find out what to do with your gold coins at
the back of the book.

With special thanks to Tabitha Jones

For Ben, Thomas and Sophia Bradford

www.beastquest.co.uk

ORCHARD BOOKS
338 Euston Road, London NW1 3BH
Orchard Books Australia
Level 17/207 Kent St, Sydney, NSW 2000

A Paperback Original
First published in Great Britain in 2015

Beast Quest is a registered trademark of Beast Quest Limited
Series created by Beast Quest Limited, London

Text © Beast Quest Limited 2015
Cover and inside illustrations by Steve Sims
© Beast Quest Limited 2015

A CIP catalogue record for this book is available from
the British Library.

ISBN 978 1 40833 493 5

1 3 5 7 9 10 8 6 4 2

Printed and bound by CPI Group (UK) Ltd, Croydon, CR0 4YY

MIX
Paper from
responsible sources
FSC® C104740

The paper and board used in this book are made from wood
from responsible sources.

Orchard Books is an imprint of Hachette Children's Group
and published by The Watts Publishing Group Limited,
an Hachette UK company.

www.hachette.co.uk

QUAGOS
THE ARMOURED BEETLE

BY ADAM BLADE

ORCHARD

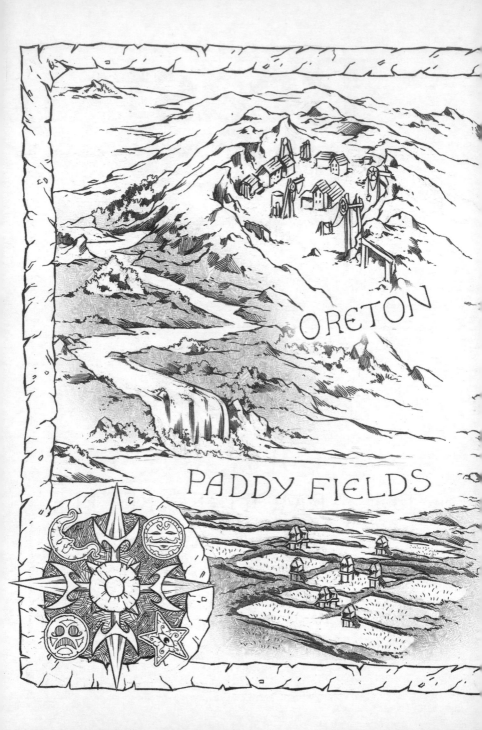

CONTENTS

Dear Reader

You join us at a moment of great historical importance. King Hugo of Avantia is about to make an official visit to our neighbours in the south, the kingdom of Tangala. Tangala was once Avantia's staunchest ally, but the kingdoms have been at odds for decades. Now, the marriage of His Majesty to Tangala's Queen Aroha will unite our kingdoms once again.

Tangala is the only kingdom in which no Beasts lurk. Powerful ancient magic protects the kingdom's borders from Evil. It is our hope that this journey should be a simple one, untouched by danger...

But things are rarely so simple.

Aduro
Former Wizard to King Hugo

PROLOGUE

Epa's six young trainees lunged and thrust, their double-edged swords glinting in the morning sun. As they danced back and forth across the palace courtyard, their faces were flushed from their efforts.

Epa the Iron Fist, Sergeant-at-Arms in the Queen's Guard, watched them with growing concern.

They're nowhere near ready to face the Avantian threat.

She flexed her broad shoulders, easing the tension in her muscles. How dare the Avantian traitors bring their dark magic to Tangala! If their warrior children hadn't stolen Queen Aroha's Treasures of Tangala, the kingdom wouldn't be in this danger now.

Epa swallowed her anger and turned her attention back to her students. Teera, the youngest, jabbed fiercely at her opponent's chest, surprising the older woman and making her stagger.

The girl shows promise, Epa thought. But Teera's blow had lacked power.

Epa crossed the yard to her student's side. "To fight takes balance," she said. "Here, like this..." But as Epa reached for Teera's wrist, a deep rumble shook the ground.

Epa drew her sword, widening her stance to keep stable. She scanned the courtyard with narrowed eyes. Red dust and small stones skittered down the palace walls as the trembling grew stronger.

"An earthquake!" Teera cried, her voice almost drowned out by the groaning from the ground.

Epa shook her head. "This is no earthquake," she said.

CRASH! Epa was thrown violently backwards as the earth

beneath her burst open.

"Get back!" she cried, waving her students towards the palace wall behind her and then scrambling to her feet. She shifted her grip on her sword and edged carefully nearer to the jagged gash that had opened in the ground, bending her knees to keep her balance. The courtyard shuddered beneath Epa's boots and the chasm gaped wider and wider. Iridescent green spikes jutted up from its depths.

The spikes rose higher, each one the size of a tree, barbed with spikes and forked at the end. A broad flat head followed from the chasm, and shiny jointed legs scrabbled at the crumbling earth,

dragging a glistening green body
out into the light. Epa glanced back
to see her young recruits huddled

against the palace wall, their swords raised and their eyes wide with terror.

Fear twisted in Epa's own stomach as she turned to face the monstrous Beast.

"Quagos?" she breathed. Every child knew the legend of the giant stag beetle, which hadn't been seen in the kingdom for a great many years. But fireside tales hadn't prepared Epa for the reality. Quagos was the size of a barn. As he clambered towards her, his huge mandibles clashed together. The eyes that bulged from each side of his massive head glowed a sickly yellow. Epa could see a shining silver rod embedded between them.

The queen's stolen sceptre! she realised. *What dark sorcery have the Avantians unleashed with it?*

Epa licked her dry lips. Her hands shook as she lifted her sword. *The first rule of battle*, she told herself. *Find your opponent's weak spot.* She scanned the beetle's glistening blue-green armour.

"Yah!" Suddenly Teera charged out from behind her towards the creature. Her sword was raised and her eyes flashed angrily.

"No!" Epa cried. But it was too late. The Beast swung its head, swiping Teera aside with a blow from its massive pincers. The young woman crumpled to the ground.

"Stay back!" Epa ordered the

others. The Beast turned a glowing yellow eye towards her. *A weak spot!* Epa thought. She gripped her broadsword in both hands, swung it back and charged.

As her feet pounded over broken paving slabs, she focussed on the weight and the power of her sword. Epa lunged, swinging her blade with all her strength. The creature's head whipped up out of reach as it reared up on its back legs. Epa's sword smashed against the Beast's shining leg armour. *Thwack!* The blow rang painfully along her arms but didn't even dent Quagos's shell.

Epa staggered back, staring up at the Beast. Her hand was sweaty on the hilt of her sword. Her heart was thumping hard. Quagos's pincers reached almost to the palace roof! His yellow eyes flashed, then his massive body toppled forwards. Epa turned and ran.

BOOM! The ground shook as the Beast crashed down behind her. Epa staggered, but managed to stay on her feet. She gritted her teeth and didn't look back.

Snap! The Beast's pincers clamped shut about her waist. Epa's stomach lurched as she was snatched upwards into the air.

She struggled against the jaws that crushed her flesh. She beat them with her sword's hilt, but it was like hammering cold steel.

Wind whipped past her and the

courtyard spun as the Beast swung its head, then let go. Epa's stomach leapt. Her arms and legs flailed in the air. She could see the courtyard wall rushing towards her. She put up her hands to protect her head and braced herself.

CRASH! Pain seared through her like lightning and thunder hitting at once, before everything around her turned to darkness.

SPRINGING THE TRAP

Tom's voice was hoarse from shouting for help. The water in the well was icy and the cold seeped into his bones. His legs ached from treading water.

A musty underground smell filled the narrow space around him, and smooth, curved brick rose up on every side. High above Tom's head, a pale circle of sky outlined the shape of a bucket hanging from a rope.

Beside him, Elenna shivered violently, her head bobbing in the water, and her hands making ripples as she paddled. Silver whimpered as he swam in circles to stay afloat.

"We can't wait here until one of the villagers finds us," Tom said. "Rotu and Velmal will be long gone by then. There has to be a way out of here!"

The Evil Wizard and treacherous prince were getting further away by the moment. And with them went the magical Treasures of Tangala that Tom and Elenna had fought three Beasts to recover.

Elenna glanced at Silver. "I don't think Silver can swim for much longer. We have to get out of here. But the walls look too smooth for us to climb."

"I could use the power of my golden boots, if only there was some solid ground to jump from." Tom said. Desperately, he looked about himself, as if a ledge might suddenly appear – but all he could see was red brick, and crumbling mortar...

Hmmm. The cracks in the mortar were barely deep enough for a fingertip. *But I have to try.*

"I've got an idea," Tom said. "Keep Silver away from the walls. I don't want to fall on either of you."

Elenna beckoned Silver. "What are

you going to do?"

"I'm going to try and climb out, but I don't know if I can."

Tom swam to the wall of the well, and scanned the brick. He found a chink in the mortar and dug his freezing fingertips into the crack. Bracing himself with his arms, Tom drew his feet towards the wall, and searched for a hold below the water with his toes.

There! The toe of one boot found a tiny ledge. Tom pulled himself upwards, grunting with the effort. *Yes!* His other foot slid into a crack. His fingers shook as he heaved himself up, finding new grips for his hands and feet. Finally, he was clear of the water. But his aching fingers wouldn't hold for long.

This had better work!

Using the power of his magic boots, Tom pushed off from the wall with his toes, throwing himself upwards and backwards. *Whoosh!* Brickwork whizzed past as he

zoomed towards the wall at his back. Tom kicked a leg out behind him just before he hit the wall, then surged up and forwards, his front leg ready to kick off again.

With two more springing leaps from wall to wall, Tom reached the top of the well. His ribs slammed the brickwork but he ignored the pain and hooked his elbows over the rim. He heaved himself up and scrambled out into daylight.

"You did it!" cried Elenna, her voice echoing upwards.

Once Tom's eyes had adjusted, he scanned the outskirts of the village around him, then looked to the horizon – but there was no sign of Velmal or Rotu.

Tom balled his fists in frustration. The thought of Velmal on the loose filled him with dread. The Evil Wizard would be using his black gemstone to control the Beast that held the last of Queen Aroha's magical Treasures.

And now Velmal has the three Treasures Rotu stole, he'll be more powerful than ever, Tom thought.

King Hugo in prison along with Daltec and Aduro; war brewing; a Beast and an Evil Wizard to defeat...

This could be my most pressing Quest yet.

"Tom?" Elenna's voice brought him back to himself. "We could really do with a hand down here!"

"I'll lower the bucket," Tom called.

He turned the handle on the side of
the well, lowering the bucket down
to Elenna. Once it was within reach,
Elenna grabbed the rope above the
bucket and wrapped it securely
about her arm.

"To me, Silver," Elenna said, then
pulled the sodden wolf close with
her free arm. "All set!" she called up.

Tom called on the strength of his
golden breastplate and turned the
well handle as fast as he could.

Before long, Elenna and Silver
cleared the brickwork. Elenna's face
was pink, and she was biting her
lip with the strain of holding Silver.
Tom reached out a hand and grabbed

the bucket, then heaved it towards
him. Silver leapt free and shook out
his coat, spattering Tom with water.
Elenna hopped down beside them,
her boots squelching as she landed.

Tom put his fingers to his mouth
and let out a long, low whistle.
Soon, he could hear the clatter of
hooves, and a moment later, Storm
cantered towards them. Tom could
see a frayed rope hanging from the
stallion's neck.

"I'm so glad you escaped from
Rotu and Velmal!" Tom said. Storm
whickered, nuzzling his soft nose
against Tom's cheek. Tom untied the
rope from Storm's neck and ran his
hand along his stallion's flank, then
turned to Elenna. "We'd better go

now. There's no time to lose."

"Indeed there isn't," said a familiar voice. Tom turned to see Daltec's magical image shimmering in the air. New worry lines were etched between the young Wizard's brows, and his hair was a tangled mess.

"Daltec!" Tom said. "Should you be risking using magic? If the Tangalans find you talking to us, they might think you are plotting against them."

"I would not have risked it," Daltec said, "except under the direst circumstances." His voice was hushed and hurried. "Tom, you must come to Pania at once. The final Beast is attacking. The palace guard is overwhelmed, and the city is in chaos. I fear that if you do not reach us soon, all will be lost." Daltec's eyes suddenly went wide, and he glanced back over his shoulder. "They're coming. I must go." He vanished.

Tom leapt up onto Storm's back, and Elenna climbed up behind him. "Rotu and Velmal can wait," Tom said. "Pania needs our help."

A CITY IN CHAOS

Tom and Elenna rode hard and fast
towards the city of Pania. Storm's
hooves flew over the barren Tangalan
desert and a hot wind buffeted them.
Tom had used his magic horseshoe
to increase Storm's speed, leaving
Silver to catch up when he could.
But a wide sea of red sand separated
them from the mountain that lifted
Pania high above the scorching

plains. *People are suffering,* Tom thought. *I need to be there!*

Finally they arrived at the foot of the mountain. Tom pulled Storm to a stop and glanced up at the city. Clouds of red dust rose like smoke from between the buildings. A dull vibration, too low to hear, shuddered through the ground.

"Can you feel that?" Elenna asked. "It's like a thousand horses running."

Tom nodded. "Or like a city being destroyed," he said. "We'd better hurry." They led Storm up the rocky path that wound around the mountain. As they climbed, a strange grating cry echoed down towards them. It was like the screech of rusted hinges, but angry and alive. Tom and Elenna exchanged a worried glance. *The Beast!*

They hurried onwards, only stopping when they reached the great stone dragons that flanked the city gates. Between the terrible cries of the Beast, Tom could hear the screams of women and children. *I hope we're not too late*, he thought. Storm pawed the red earth, snorting.

Elenna was pale. "We need to get in and help!" she said. But the gates were barred.

Tom put his hand to the red jewel in his belt. The terrible shrieking became a hideous, gleeful voice.

Flee as fast as you can, people of Pania, it cried. *Flee from Quagos!*

Quagos, Tom thought. *Soon you'll*

be wishing you *could flee!* He ran his
eyes along the solid city walls. There
was no way in except for the gate.

"Wait here with Storm," Tom told
Elenna. "I am going to send my
shadow ahead to look inside." Elenna
nodded, and Tom pressed a fingertip
to the white jewel in his belt. He felt
a sliding sensation, as if the earth
was slipping out from under him.
When it stopped, he was standing
beside his own frozen body, feeling
as light as air. Tom's shadow-self
drifted forwards, pressing through
thick wood of the closed gates.

Tom found himself in a square
surrounded by sandstone buildings

and filled with market stalls and carts. At the back, the red turrets and domes of the queen's sandstone palace rose above the city.

Many of the buildings in the square bore long, jagged cracks. The canopies of the market stalls were ripped, and food and other goods covered the ground. People were running in all directions, their faces twisted with terror. At the heart of the chaos, standing tall on his jointed hind legs, Quagos lifted his pincer-like mandibles and let out a terrific screech. Something silver embedded between the Beast's glowing yellow eyes caught the sun.

The queen's sceptre!

Tom had seen enough. He called his

shadow back to his body.

"The Beast is rampaging,"Tom told Elenna. "If we don't get in there now, Pania will be destroyed." He called on the strength of his golden breastplate and took a deep breath, focussing his power. Then he ran at the gate and slammed his shoulder hard into its wooden planks.

Thud! The gate shuddered. Tom took a few steps back, then charged again. *Smash!* There was the sharp crack of splintering wood as Tom's shoulder exploded with pain. He stood back again, then ran forward once more.

CRASH! The gates flew open and Tom tumbled inside, grabbing his throbbing shoulder.

"Silver!" Elenna cried. Tom turned
to see the wolf arrive at her side, his
tongue lolling and his sides heaving.

Elenna bent to let Silver lick her
face. "You must have run like the
wind to catch up so fast," she said.
She straightened and ran through

the broken gate with the animals.

A woman cried, "Seize them!"

Tom spun to see six huge, leather-clad Tangalan warriors glaring down at him from just a few paces away. Their faces were streaked with dirt and their muscled arms were covered with bruises and scratches. Some wore bandages, dark with blood, and each carried a sword as broad as Tom's hand and as long as he was tall. The woman who had spoken had fierce grey eyes, a square jaw and dark hair bound back from her face. A red gash peeped from under a fraying bandage across her forehead.

The woman looked at the broken gates, then back at Tom as Quagos let out a mighty screech. Her nostrils flared with rage.

"As if you hadn't done enough damage, stealing Treasures and conjuring Beasts," the woman cried. "You're going to the cell!"

"No!" Tom said, raising his hands as the soldiers pressed towards them. "I swear to you, we neither stole those jewels nor brought that Beast. You must let us challenge Quagos. We're the only people that can defeat him." Over the woman's shoulder Tom saw Quagos swipe a water trough into the air with his jaws. A trader screamed as the trough crashed into his stall.

"Don't trust him, Epa!" a soldier cried. "They're lying sorcerers."

"We're not!" Elenna said, stepping

forward. "We're sworn to defend the innocent just like you are. Tom's saved our people from Beasts many times. He's your only hope."

There was a cracking sound from the square as Quagos uprooted a tree, which flew past them and slammed into the city wall with a thud. A flicker of uncertainty crossed Epa's face. She grimaced, then turned to Tom. "If you can defeat that monster, do it now!" she said. At a signal from Epa, the soldiers behind her parted, clearing a path to the Beast.

Tom drew his sword. "Cover me," he told Elenna. Then he strode towards the giant beetle, dropping one hand to the red jewel in his belt. *Quagos!* Tom told the Beast. *It is time you picked on someone who knows how to handle a Beast!*

Quagos froze, then turned his huge body towards Tom, feelers twitching.

Tom stared into the Beast's glassy eyes. Quagos gazed back, unmoving.

"Well! Come on, then!" Tom shouted, waving his sword.

Quagos slowly bent his long front legs and lowered his head to the ground. *What's he doing?* Tom wondered. *Is he preparing to charge?* But Quagos remained bowed.

Angry murmurs rose from the soldiers behind Tom.

Yes...yesss...good... Tom heard a voice through Torgor's red jewel.

Velmal!

Treat the boy as your master, the Dark Wizard told Quagos, *and the people will treat him as their enemy!*

So the Wizard is here, somewhere, Tom thought, preparing to charge. But before he could move, Epa leapt between him and the Beast.

"I knew it!" she cried, her huge
broadsword pointed at Tom's chest.
"You Avantians are in league with
Evil. You command the Beast!"
Sergeant Epa turned to the soldiers
behind her. "Arrest them!"

3

PRISONERS

Elenna turned her bow towards the
angry woman, but Tom shook his
head. He sheathed his sword slowly
as Elenna lowered her weapon.
Quagos scuttled backwards, his
head still bowed low to the ground.
They're letting him get away! Tom
thought. But there was nothing he
could do with Epa's sword pressed
against his ribs.

His arms were tugged roughly behind his back by a thick-set warrior woman. Another seized his sword. Elenna was dragged to his side, and Tom felt the cool touch of metal about his wrist. They were handcuffed together, his right arm to her left.

He felt a sharp shove in his back and stumbled forward with Elenna at his side. A tall, freckled woman grabbed his free arm. A grating screech cut the air, followed by a boom. Tom glanced back to see Quagos striking at a building with his jaws.

"Hurry!" Epa called to her troops. "We need to get rid of these traitors so we can defend the city!"

Tom and Elenna were shoved towards the massive palace that towered over the square. It was richly decorated with pointed spires and elegant stained-glass windows, but many of the spires were broken and the windows were laced with cracks. They passed a deep chasm that ran across the courtyard and towards an arched entrance flanked by guards.

The guards stood aside as Epa approached. Tom and Elenna were thrust through the archway after her. It opened into a long vaulted chamber hung with tapestries and lit with torches in golden sconces.

The air inside was cool. Whispering voices and shuffling footsteps echoed around the hall, along with the muffled thuds of Quagos still rampaging outside. *I should be out there fighting!* Tom thought.

At the back of the room, carpeted stairs led up to a sandstone throne surrounded by the queen's red-robed advisors and a pair of armoured guards. Queen Aroha sat raised above them, dressed in rose-gold armour studded with glittering emeralds. Her fair hair was twisted into long plaits twined with gold that shone in the light from the candles and stained-glass windows. Her delicate features and green eyes were expressionless as they rested on

Tom and Elenna.

"Your Majesty!" Epa cried. "We have captured the Avantian traitors. Quagos even bowed before the boy!"

"Bring them to me," Aroha said, in a low voice.

Tom found himself lifted off his feet and dragged towards the throne past rows of hostile eyes.

Only the queen's pale face was calm. "Explain yourselves," she said.

Tom bowed his head.

"Your Majesty," he said. "We came to you in peace, to unite our kingdoms and serve you with honour. Our enemy Velmal has escaped Grashkor's prison island and released Beasts upon your kingdom. Let us stop him, as we have before."

The queen arched an eyebrow.
"Why should we trust you?" she
demanded.

"By my honour as an Avantian, I
am telling the truth," said Tom.

"An Avantian's word is worth
nothing," said a scornful voice. Tom

recognised it at once. *Rotu!* The prince stepped from behind a long tapestry on the wall to the right of the throne. Tom balled his fists, fighting to control his rage.

Rotu shot Tom a smug look, then dropped to his knees before the queen. After bowing his head, he opened a leather satchel and carefully drew out the magic crown, ring and orb that he had stolen from Storm's saddlebag.

"Your Majesty," the prince said, laying the magical items before her, "I retrieved your Treasures from the villainous Avantians." Rotu shot Tom another smirk.

"He's lying," Elenna protested. "He's in league with Velmal!"

"Silence!" said the queen.

Tom's nails were digging into his palms hard enough to draw blood. *I mustn't let him get to me*, he told himself. *Arguing will only worsen the situation.*

"Thank you, Rotu," Aroha said more calmly to her nephew. She gestured to one of her guards. The woman stepped forward and gathered the Treasures, placing them on a table by the queen. Aroha turned her cool, green gaze back to Tom and Elenna.

"As you see, my nephew has a different version of events," she said. "One that I am inclined to believe, since he has brought back three of the precious Treasures I need to

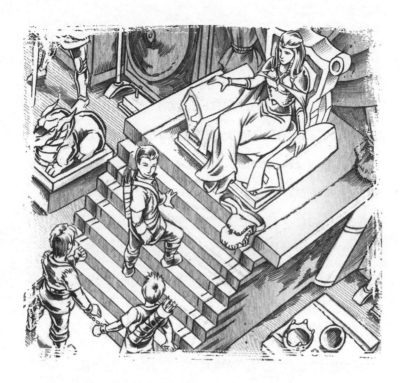

protect my kingdom."

The prince rose and turned to the
queen's red-robed counsellors with a
self-satisfied grin.

From outside, Tom could hear
thuds and screams of terror. *Rotu is
acting like Tangala's saviour, while*

*the city's being destroyed. He should
be out there fighting the Beast!*

The queen's counsellors were
muttering and casting angry glances
at Tom and Elenna. A small woman
with sharp eyes and skin as wizened
as a dried apple shook her fist.
"The Avantian children must be
imprisoned with their treacherous
king," she cried.

Aroha frowned at the mention
of the king. Uncertainty flickered
across her face. Tom could see that
she was torn. *She doesn't want to
think ill of King Hugo,* Tom realised.
*Maybe we can convince her after
all!* He stepped forward, but at that
moment, there was a terrific crash
from outside. The queen's face went

pale and her hands tightened on the arms of her chair. She closed her eyes, just for a moment, but when she opened them, they were fierce.

"Sergeant-at-Arms," she said to Epa, "these two children sealed their fate when they took the Treasures, unleashing this terror on our city. Take them to their cells."

"No!" Tom cried desperately. "The city will be destroyed!"

But Epa nodded to her soldiers. Hands grabbed hold of Tom, and shoved him and Elenna forwards.

4

A FIGHT FOR FREEDOM

The guards pushed Tom and Elenna
out through a narrow door at
the back of the room into a long
windowless corridor, lit by flickering
torches. They were marched along,
and then down steep steps to
another, darker corridor tunnelled
into the rock of the mountain. Rough
wooden doors ran along either side.

Many were open, showing dark cells within. Others were shut and barred.

The handcuff on Tom's wrist bit into his flesh with every step. Glancing at Elenna, he saw she was thinking hard. Tom's own mind was racing. He couldn't run for it using his golden boots, because Elenna would never keep up. He looked at Epa, striding ahead. *I have to try something*, he thought. *People will perish if that Beast isn't stopped.*

"Sergeant Epa," Tom said.

"Quiet!" Epa snapped back.

"It's a mistake," Tom said. "We're your only hope of saving the city."

Epa spun around and the soldier holding Tom's arm pulled up with a jolt. "Do you think I'm a fool?"

Epa said, scowling. "What do they call you? Master of the Beasts? Well, Quagos certainly seemed to treat you like a master! Our only hope of saving our city is getting rid of you Avantians once and for all!"

Tom was dragged away behind Epa. Frustration swelled in his chest. The sergeant clearly wanted to protect her people, just as he did.

We should be allies, Tom thought. *I wish I didn't have to do this...*

He called on the magic of his golden breastplate, feeling strength surge through his muscles.

"Be ready," he hissed in Elenna's ear. Tom took another step, then shoved Elenna hard to the right, cannoning her into the guard that held her. The woman's cry echoed through the tunnel as she stumbled and fell. Tom lunged left, smashing into his own guard and knocking her to the ground.

Epa spun, her sword drawn and her eyes flashing with fury.

Tom raised his manacled hand, pulling Elenna's up with it.

"Now!" Tom cried. Tom harnessed the power of his golden boots and charged forwards, pulling Elenna with him. He whipped their handcuffs up over Epa's sword, smashing the heavy chain into her chest. Epa was upended, landing with a thud on her back. Her head cracked against the flagstones and her eyes rolled shut.

Tom heard the swish of steel parting the air behind him. He and Elenna whirled, and Tom lifted the chain as a soldier charged towards them, her sword slicing downwards.

Ching! The soldier's blade sliced cleanly through the chain, setting Tom and Elenna free. The soldier

staggered forwards under the weight of her own blow. Tom lifted his manacled wrist and sent it crashing down against the hilt of her sword, knocking it from her hand.

"No!" the guard cried, scrambling after her weapon, but Tom pounced forwards and snatched it up.

The huge sword felt clumsy in his hands. *If only Epa had left me my own blade!* Tom thought, lifting the heavy broadsword high. Torchlight flickered along its length as he turned and pointed it towards the final guard, who had rounded on Elenna.

"Drop your weapon!" Tom cried. The guard looked uncertainly at Epa, lying prone on the ground, then at her injured colleague.

"Never!" she said. She lunged towards Tom. At the same time, Tom leapt high using his boots' power, and landed beside Epa. He pointed his long sword at the sergeant's throat.

"Drop your weapon," he repeated. The guard gritted her teeth, but let the sword fall. It hit the floor with a *clang*, and Elenna picked it up.

Epa groaned and her eyelids flickered open. She frowned in confusion, then her eyes focussed on the blade pointed at her throat.

"I am sorry," Tom told her, feeling a stab of guilt. "You left me no choice. But while there is blood in my veins, I will rid Tangala of this final Beast."

Epa closed her eyes in pain.

"Let's go!" Tom said. He turned

and raced back along the corridor they had followed, with Elenna at his side. Behind him, he could hear Epa's soldiers calling her name.

"We have to get out of here fast," he said. "It won't be long before the soldiers raise the alarm."

"Do you think we should free the king?" Elenna asked, glancing at the doors that lined the corridor.

"Don't!" a familiar voice called from behind a door to their left.

Tom rushed towards it. "Daltec, are you all right?"

"We are," King Hugo's voice replied. "But we cannot risk angering the queen further. We must stay until her jewels are returned and Pania is safe."

Tom frowned. He didn't like leaving

the king in prison, but he understood. *If my Quest fails, and the queen finds the king gone, nothing will prevent war between Tangala and Avantia.*

"We will return for you," Tom told his friends, "once Quagos is defeated and Avantia's future queen is safe!"

EVIL IN THEIR MIDST

Tom and Elenna peered out into the throne room, hardly daring to breathe. They had hidden behind the tapestry from which Rotu had emerged. It covered a small alcove, just big enough for them to stand in.

A muscled, grey-haired woman with tanned skin and emerald-studded armour stood before the throne. Queen Aroha sat with Rotu at her side, surrounded by a crowd of red-robed counsellors. All were leaning forward, listening to the armoured woman over the sounds of Quagos rampaging outside.

"Recruits have been summoned from all over Tangala," she said. "They're being trained by our very best. We will conquer this Beast. And when we do, we will be ready to strike back at Avantia. As long as their treacherous king is imprisoned here, our attack will surprise their troops. We can remove the threat of their evil magic once and for all!"

Queen Aroha's brows were pinched together. She put her fingers to her temples. "It doesn't make sense!" she said softly. "Hugo has always been an honourable man – and a friend! I can't believe he is behind all of this."

The keen-eyed elder who had demanded Tom and Elenna's imprisonment stepped forward.

"You cannot risk trusting him, Your Majesty," she said. "Hugo stands to rule two kingdoms by marrying you. Mark my words, power changes people. I have seen it many times. Hugo's Beast is destroying our city. You must act now!" As if to underline her point, a bang from outside shook the palace walls.

Quagos is getting closer!

"She speaks the truth!" Rotu cried. "I have said it all along – Hugo is tired of ruling his pathetic little kingdom. He thinks his Beast will scare us into submission. But he underestimates our courage and strength! War will show him that we cannot be defeated so easily."

Elenna drew a sharp breath and Tom felt his own temper flaring. But they had to stay silent. For now.

The queen sighed heavily, shaking her head. "War means death and famine and sorrow," she said. "It is a last resort for when all else has failed." There were dark circles under her eyes. She looked sad and tired and worried. But Tom felt a spark of hope. Aroha did not want war... *Which means we have a chance!*

Tom heard a sudden hiss of fury and impatience. One of the queen's advisors stepped forward.

"Weak!" the man cried. "You fools couldn't start a fire in a volcano!" There was a gasp of outrage from the other advisors as the man threw back his hood, revealing sharp features and cruel black eyes.

Velmal!

Elenna started forward, but Tom grabbed her arm. "Wait!" Tom hissed. "Let Velmal show himself for the wicked impostor he is."

"I'll just have to take matters into my own hands!" the Wizard snapped. He snatched up the queen's magical jewels from the table at her side.

Aroha tried to grab his wrist, but he darted out of reach.

"Seize him!" the queen cried. Her

guards darted after the Evil Wizard
as he streaked across the room
towards a stained-glass window.
Velmal lifted the queen's crown and
sent it crashing through the glass.
Sunlight streamed through the
shattered window, catching Velmal's

black stone as he held it high.

The Wizard's lips moved in an incantation and his eyes flashed with triumph as the guards ran towards him. *No!* Tom thought. *He's calling the Beast with his magic jewel!*

"What are you doing?" Rotu shouted. His face was white and his eyes were wide and panicked as the whole room shuddered. The guards advancing on Velmal staggered and fell. Cracks zigzagged down the walls and the furniture rattled.

Tom gripped the hilt of his sword and squared his shoulders. Velmal had summoned Quagos. The time for stealth and secrecy was over.

The Beast was coming and Tom was ready.

6

TOM MAKES A PROMISE

Tom watched from behind the tapestry, waiting for the right moment to strike. Rotu's lips were quivering as his eyes darted around the quaking room. "This wasn't the deal!" he told Velmal in a panicked voice. "You weren't supposed to destroy the city! You were supposed to make the Avantians look like a threat so I could drive them away!"

Velmal curled his lip in disgust. "Can you really be that stupid?" he snarled. "Evil Wizards only seek the help of vain fools and cowards – they are far more easily tricked into betraying their friends!"

Rotu staggered back as if he had been hit. Tom felt a stab of pity for the prince – but he felt anger too. *Rotu has put his whole kingdom at risk for his own ambition!*

The queen's face was flushed with fury and her green eyes sparked as she stared at her nephew. "I expected far better from you," she said. Then she pointed towards Velmal. "Take him!" she cried.

Velmal grinned as the guards

scrabbled across the shifting floor towards him. He already had one foot on the windowsill.

You're not getting away that easily! Tom burst from behind the tapestry and lunged towards the Evil Wizard with Elenna at his side. They raced across the room, but at the sound of their footsteps, the guards turned and lifted their swords, blocking their path.

"No!" Tom cried, pointing towards the window. But it was too late. Velmal leapt through the smashed glass, his cape flaring behind him, and vanished into the courtyard below. "Let me pass!" Tom urged the guards. "I must stop Quagos before he destroys the palace!"

Aroha gestured to her guards. "Let me speak with the boy," she said. The guards lowered their weapons and drew apart.

Tom stepped forwards and dropped to one knee at Aroha's feet, bowing his head. Elenna did the same. When Tom lifted his eyes, the queen held his gaze. The terrible sounds of destruction and fear were echoing all around them. Long cracks were running across the palace floor.

"Do you know you can defeat this Beast?" she asked.

Queen Aroha is just and wise, Tom thought. *She will see the truth.*

"Your Majesty," Tom said. "No one can win every battle. My father died protecting Avantia, and I know that my own death will come one day at the hand of a Beast. But I can promise you, I will do my best to make sure this is not that day."

The queen nodded. "Go, then," she said. She reached out her hand and laid it gently on Tom's shoulder. "And may the blessings of my kingdom go with you."

Tom turned to Elenna. "Ready?" he said. Elenna lifted her sword and nodded. They took a step back, then ran towards the window. Tom leapt first through the shattered glass and into the courtyard below.

Elenna landed beside him. They scanned the scene. Quagos was lashing at the palace walls with his

heavy, armoured jaws. The walls
were cracked, but they were holding
– just. The queen's guards had
formed a line and were advancing
on the Beast from behind.

Tom turned away and ran his
eyes over the wide, rubble-strewn

courtyard that opened into the square, leading to the city walls.

"There!" Elenna said, pointing. Tom followed the line of her finger and spotted a red-cloaked form streaking from behind a shattered cart towards the city gates.

Velmal.

"Watch my back!" Tom said. "Without Velmal and his jewel commanding him, Quagos should be weak enough to defeat."

Tom called on the magic of his golden leg armour and launched himself forward. He raced over the dusty ground, leaping over fallen bricks and debris, keeping his eyes focussed on Velmal's retreating form.

As Tom drew close to the red-

cloaked Wizard, he ducked one
shoulder and barrelled forwards.

SMACK! Tom's shoulder smashed
into Velmal's back, knocking him off
his feet. The Wizard flew through
the air and landed with a thud.
He started to scramble up but
Tom lunged, kicking Velmal's feet
from under him and sending him
sprawling into the dust. Tom sprang
over his fallen enemy and turned the
point of his broadsword downwards
to rest on Velmal's chest.

"Give me the jewel that controls
the Beasts," Tom ordered.

Velmal curled his lip in a snarl,
then opened his mouth to speak.

"Tom!" Elenna's breathless
cry reached him from across the

courtyard. The ground beneath his feet began to shake. "Quagos is coming your way!"

7

BATTLING THE BEAST

Tom glanced over his shoulder to
see Quagos lurching across the
courtyard towards him. The giant
beetle swung his jaws left and right
as he moved, sending the queen's
soldiers flying as they tried to
hold him back with their swords.
The Beast's massive body tipped
and jerked as his armoured limbs

clambered over fallen rubble. As his yellow eyes rested on Tom, his pincer-like jaws chomped together hungrily. Tom glanced down at Velmal. The Wizard was smirking.

"Ha! My Beast will crush you and the city to dust!" Velmal said, his eyes filled with ravenous glee. "You will be—"

SMACK! Tom slammed his fist hard into the side of the Wizard's skull. Velmal's sneering voice fell silent and his eyes rolled closed.

"I'll deal with you later!" Tom said. Then he turned towards the Beast. Quagos was almost upon him, a hulking mass of shining green armour as strong as steel. Elenna was racing towards the creature with her sword raised while soldiers advanced from either side. Tom lifted his awkward blade, wishing again that he had his own familiar sword to use.

But a warrior must make do with whatever weapon he has to hand.

Quagos put on a burst of speed,

racing ahead of Elenna and the queen's troops, his flat head lowered as he charged at Tom with a grating shriek. The sound was so loud and so terrible the soldiers stopped and slapped their hands over their ears, grimacing in pain.

Tom stood his ground as the Beast drew close. The creature's jaws opened wide, and its yellow eyes flashed. Tom could see every detail of the queen's silver sceptre glinting in the Beast's flat, ram-like head. The ground shook with each step that Quagos took. Tom called on the power of his golden boots and leapt upwards, soaring over Quagos's crushing pincers and landing in a crouch on the Beast's shining armour. It was as smooth and cold as polished stone.

Tom scrambled forwards until he reached the sceptre embedded between the creature's glowing eyes. Quagos shook his head and Tom dropped to his knees to stop himself being flung into the air. He prised at the sceptre with his fingers, trying

to dig it out as Quagos's body tipped and jerked beneath him. It was no use. There was no way to get a hold. Tom lifted his sword, wondering if he could use its point to free the sceptre from the Beast's armour.

But Quagos lifted his head and reared. Tom's stomach lurched as his feet slid out from under him. He crashed down onto Quagos's back, barely managing to keep his grip on his sword.

"Hold on, Tom!" Elenna cried. "I'm coming!" Tom scrabbled with his toes and free hand, trying to find a grip, but the shell was too smooth. *I have to get that sceptre!* he thought.

Quagos jerked his head even higher, sending Tom tumbling backwards.

CRASH! Tom's back thudded against the ground. His head whipped back and hit the earth. White light exploded behind his eyes. Tom shook his head gingerly. When his vision cleared, Quagos was rearing high on his hind legs, towering over him. Tom could see nothing but the Beast's reddish underbelly rising up and up.

He's going to crush me!

"Take that!" Elenna yelled. Tom heard a sharp crack, and Quagos screeched in pain. His massive body jerked sideways. Tom glanced between the creature's hind legs to see Elenna swinging back her sword, her face red and streaked with dirt. She gave a cry and hacked again at the soft joint in Quagos's leg. Tom saw the knee joint buckle. His heart thundered in his chest as the giant beetle plummeted towards him. Tom hurled himself aside with all his strength and kept rolling.

BOOM! Quagos landed beside him with a force that shook the mountain. As Tom rolled to a stop, he could see Elenna scrambling up beside the Beast's damaged hind leg. All around them the square was filled with cries of panic and the sound of falling rocks.

Tom got to his feet as the giant beetle heaved its vast belly off the ground. He aimed a hefty blow at

Quagos's shell, but his blade simply glanced off.

Quagos swung his huge body around. As Tom scrambled out of the way of the creature's crushing feet, he saw the Beast's glowing eyes come to rest on Elenna. Quagos opened his jaws wide, preparing to attack. Tom hacked at the creature's shell from behind, but it was no use. Tangalan soldiers were swarming in from either side firing crossbows, but their arrows merely pinged harmlessly off the Beast's armour.

Elenna stood firm, her sword raised in both hands.

I have to help her! Tom darted between the creature's legs and under its body. He lifted his sword

and slashed hard at the flesh of the
beetle's underbelly. His sharp sword
scored a long, straight cut which
instantly oozed green blood.

Quagos shuddered and shrieked
as Tom dived out from under him.
The huge creature's feelers twitched
wildly as he thrashed his head in
agony. Elenna leapt back, barely
dodging a swipe from the creature's

mighty jaws. Tom wasn't so lucky.
He heard a swoosh of air, then his
feet were swept from the ground by
a tremendous blow to his ribs. He
surged upwards, sailing over broken
stalls and rubble towards the red
sandstone wall of the palace...

8

TODAY IS NOT THAT DAY

CRASH!

Shards of coloured glass exploded all around Tom as he smashed through the palace window. His shoulder hit the ground with a crack and his head thumped against something hard. Tom slumped in pain. He licked his lips and tasted blood.

When he opened his eyes, light

seared into his brain like a knife. He tried to lift his head, his arms…but his limbs felt like they belonged to someone else.

Tom could hear Elenna shouting outside…the clang of her sword and the terrible screech of the Beast.

No! I can't let her fight alone.

Tom took a deep breath, gritted his teeth and pushed himself up on his elbow, waiting for the dizziness to subside. He could feel his strength returning. He stood up slowly, fragments of coloured glass falling from his clothes as crossed to the broken window.

Outside, Elenna was fighting beside Epa and her soldiers. They were hacking at the Beast with their

swords. But Quagos was deflecting their blows almost effortlessly.

Time for a surprise attack! Tom thought. He called on the power of his golden breastplate and felt a swell of energy inside him. He gripped his sword, and leapt back through the broken window. Tom landed with a jolt, steadied himself, then called on the power of his golden boots. He hurled himself forwards, racing across the courtyard.

The Beast was busy warding off Epa and Elenna's blows. Tom powered towards it. He focussed the magical strength of his breastplate into his arms and gripped his broadsword in both hands. Tom swung back his sword and sent it in a wide arc towards the soft darkness at the bend in the Beast's good back leg.

THWACK! The Beast's leg buckled. Quagos tipped back his head and let out a scream like steel scraping stone. The sound sliced through Tom's aching head, making him gasp with pain. But Elenna and Epa were ready.

"Stay back!" Epa called to her troops. Elenna and Epa lifted their swords and charged, one at each of the Beast's front legs. Their swords bit into Quagos's jointed knees. As the Beast fell, they darted out of reach.

Quagos was leaning at an angle, barely supporting his massive weight above the ground. He screamed in anger and pain, his feelers twisting about wildly. Four of his legs were bent and broken. Two jointed legs remained intact.

Tom lunged forwards, his sword biting into flesh. Quagos's remaining good legs buckled. Tom jumped back as the Beast's huge body crashed down, almost crushing him. The ground shook with the weight of the

Beast as Tom called once more on the magic of his golden boots.

Tom somersaulted, landing on the Beast's glistening, armoured shell. He could see Epa and Elenna below him, their swords raised and ready. Tom lifted his own blade in both

hands, with its sharp tip pointing downwards. He focussed on the narrow groove that ran between the Beast's glistening wings, calling on the power of his amber jewel, which enhanced his sword-fighting skills.

Then he sent his sword plunging

downwards. *CRACK!* A split ran along the Beast's body, all the way to its head. Tom felt Quagos jerk once, then freeze. He glanced towards the Armoured Beetle's head and saw the feelers shudder and stop still, as if they had been turned to stone. The pale yellow glow of Quagos's bulging eyes flickered and went out. *Time to get off!* Tom thought. He leapt from the Beast's back and turned, just in time to see the green shell collapse in on itself, creasing and crumpling down to a tiny point. In less than a heartbeat, all that was left was a glimmer of silver. Queen Aroha's sceptre fell and landed next to Tom.

Tom held it high to show to Elenna and Epa. "Tangala is saved—"

"Look out!" Elenna cried, pointing behind him. Tom started to turn but strong hands thudded into his side, knocking him from his feet and hurling him to the ground. Tom's broadsword and the queen's sceptre flew from his hands as he fell. He rolled, his fingers already reaching for his fallen weapon, but a red-cloaked figure leapt over and booted it away.

Velmal grinned down at Tom, his craggy face filled with hate. In one hand he held a leather bag, while in the other was the queen's crown.

"Sorry to disappoint you," the Wizard said, "but I have three magical tokens and a jewel that controls the Beasts. With or without Quagos, you're not going to beat me now!"

9

THE WARRIOR QUEEN

Velmal pulled back his arm and sent the queen's jewel-encrusted crown smashing down towards Tom's face. Tom rolled, dodging the crown and grabbing for his sword. His fingers curled around the hilt, but Velmal's boot stomped down on the blade, pinning it to the ground. Tom scrambled up, leaving his sword and lifting his fists instead.

"You will pay for your treachery!"
Epa shouted, storming across the
courtyard towards the Evil Wizard.
Elenna was at her side, her sword
pulled back ready to strike.

Velmal lifted the hand that held
the crown and grinned. "One more
step and I'll crush this pretty
trinket," he said. Epa and Elenna
froze. Tom scanned the Wizard's face.
His dark eyes shone with menace.

He'll do it, Tom thought, dropping
his fists.

"Ha!" Velmal cried. "I always knew
I'd get the better of you." But as
Velmal grinned wickedly, Tom saw
something dart across the courtyard
towards them. A slender figure clad

in gleaming rose-gold was surging straight towards Velmal's back.

The queen!

"For Tangala!" Aroha cried in a high, clear voice.

She lifted her leg and landed a flying kick at the base of the Wizard's

spine. Velmal sprawled to the ground, dropping the crown. His cloak tangled about him as he rolled, but he scrambled to his feet. Epa darted forward and picked up the crown. Tom and Elenna leapt towards the Wizard but Aroha beat them to it.

She drew her gleaming sword and pointed it at Velmal's heart. "Give me the rest of my Treasures!" she commanded fiercely.

Velmal's scowl deepened. He lifted the bag with the Treasures and held it out to Aroha. But as the queen extended her hand, the Wizard pulled back and threw the bag straight into her face. The queen cried out and Epa ran to her side. Tom lunged for Velmal, swinging his

fist. Quick as a snake, Velmal leapt
back and slipped his hand inside his
robe. He whipped out a glass vial
and dashed it to the ground.

BANG!

Thick, purple-grey smoke billowed
up, filling the air with a sickly sweet
smell and blinding Tom completely.
He groped with his hands, trying
to find the Wizard, but he caught
hold of nothing but purple fog. He
could hear the sound of Epa's heavy
footsteps, and Elenna's swift ones
scuffling the ground as they both
searched for Velmal. He could also
hear soft leather boots running away.

Tom raced towards the sound,

reaching out in the fog. His fingertips brushed thick folds of fabric, and Tom lunged and grabbed. His arms closed around Velmal's broad chest. The Wizard swung his head back.

Crunch!

"Aargh!" Tom felt his nose shatter, his body buckling from the blow. He let go of Velmal and stumbled back, his hands clasped to his face as blood gushed through his fingers. He blinked away the water in his eyes to see the purple fog was clearing. Velmal was racing across the courtyard with Epa and Elenna hot on his heels.

But the queen was ahead of them, her sword glinting in the sun. Tom stumbled forwards after the others, his head spinning and drops of blood from his injured nose darkening the red earth as he ran.

"You won't get away so easily!" Aroha cried, lifting her sword. The Dark Wizard spun in a swirl of red.

No! Tom thought, watching Velmal snatch out a hand to grip the queen's wrist, twisting it until she dropped her gleaming blade. Elenna and Epa pounded towards the Wizard, Tom running as fast as he could.

Velmal bent to scoop up the fallen weapon and place its blade against Aroha's throat.

"Drop your weapons, or she dies!" Velmal snarled. Epa and Elenna pulled up before him. Tom froze where he was.

"Get away from my aunt!" a furious voice cried.

Rotu?

The prince flew towards Velmal, wielding Aroha's silver sceptre like a club, and smashed it against the side of the Wizard's skull.

Velmal cried out and staggered sideways, losing his grip on the queen. Aroha fell forwards, clutching her throat, but Rotu caught her.

"Your Majesty! Are you hurt?" he asked. The queen lifted her head and nodded weakly.

Velmal was already racing towards the courtyard wall. Tom pounded after him.

"Stop, traitor!" Rotu shouted.

Soon he was running at Tom's side.
But Velmal lifted his hand and let
something fall behind him. *Another
vial!* There was a soft *pop*, and
the air was instantly filled with
a choking, burning yellow fog.

Tom coughed and gasped. Rotu stumbled and fell to his knees clawing at his throat. Tom staggered forward another step, then fell too, struggling for breath. He could hear Epa and Elenna behind him, wheezing and gagging.

As the fog began to clear, Tom saw Rotu getting unsteadily to his feet. Tom stood beside him, scanning the courtyard for Velmal. He saw a flash of red disappear through a crack in the city wall, and gritted his teeth.

"We must catch him!" Rotu cried in a hoarse voice. He stumbled forwards, but he was dizzy with the smoke and almost fell. Tom caught his arm.

"Let him go," Tom said. "He won't

be able to get far. The important thing is, Tangala is saved, and the Treasures are back where they belong. We'll deal with Velmal later. That's a promise."

10

AN UNINVITED GUEST

Tom looked himself up and down in the gilt-framed mirror before him. Clean and rested, he looked almost smart in the blue silk tunic and velveteen breeches he'd been given to wear to the wedding. Except for his bruises and scratches. And the broken nose, of course!

Tom grinned. "It's a good thing

Tangala is protected from Beasts again," he said, turning away from the mirror, to where Elenna stood in the corner. "I don't fancy our chances at fighting dressed like this!"

"Hmph!" Elenna replied, scowling and fiddling with the ribbon that had been tied in her short, spiky hair. Her dress had puffy bows at the shoulders and a ruffled skirt.

"Can you pass me the green jewel?" Tom asked, running a finger along the crooked bridge of his nose.

Elenna frowned as she picked up Tom's jewelled belt from his bed. "Are you sure you want to mend your nose?" she asked, grinning at him. "I quite like it how it is. It's funny the way it curves in two directions at once." Then she burst out laughing.

Tom started to join in, but then winced in pain. With a broken nose, laughing was painful!

"I'm glad you find it so amusing," he said. "But it really hurts!"

"Oh, go on then," Elenna said, handing him the green jewel.

Tom took it, and held the smooth jewel to his nose. He heard a gristly click, then let out a long sigh of relief. "Now that feels better!"

"Well, if you're ready," Elenna said, "we'd better go." She cocked her elbow towards him and fluttered her eyelids jokingly. Tom grinned, and hooked his arm into hers.

They made their way out of the palace and towards the banqueting

tent, taking slow, dignified steps, and suppressing giggles the whole way.

The palace courtyard was packed with finely dressed people hurrying to the royal wedding. Most of the debris that Quagos had created had already been cleared away. The banqueting tent was right at the back, pitched against the city wall.

Tom could hear chattering voices from inside. Epa stood guard at the door of the tent. She bowed, blushing, as Tom and Elenna approached her. Tom stuck out his hand, and Epa grinned and shook it warmly. Then Tom and Elenna slipped inside.

They made their way through the throng of people to stand beside Daltec and Aduro. Daltec was clean for the first time in days, and dressed in a long purple cloak. Aduro looked as wise and dignified as ever in silver and green. They both turned to smile as Tom and Elenna took their places in the row of seats behind them.

Suddenly, Daltec's smile turned to a scowl. Tom looked over his shoulder to see Prince Rotu hurrying towards him.

"Just what we need," Elenna hissed to Tom.

Rotu frowned nervously as he moved to stand before Tom and Elenna, then he dropped his eyes and looked at his hands. "I... I wanted to apologise. For everything. I was such a fool. And I..."

Tom put out a hand and rested it on Rotu's shoulder. The prince lifted his eyes.

"What's done is done," Tom said gently. "I know how persuasive Evil

Wizards can be. You made a mistake. You learned your lesson. There's nothing more to say." Rotu smiled gratefully. Tom offered his hand, and Rotu shook it. Elenna stuck her hand out as well, with only a trace of a scowl. Rotu shook hers too, then ducked away to take his own place near the front of the tent.

Elenna frowned as she watched him go. "So why is the wedding taking place out here near the city walls, instead of in the banqueting hall?" she asked. "Surely the palace would have been safer – what if Velmal returns?"

"Don't worry," said Tom. "Daltec and I have made plans..."

"What plans?" asked Elenna,

raising an eyebrow.

Tom was about to answer when an angry cry went up from the crowd, followed by shouts of alarm. Elegantly dressed guests bumped into each other as a cloaked figure pushed through their midst. The figure burst from the crowd, threw back his hood and darted towards the prince.

"Velmal!" Elenna hissed, starting forward. But Tom caught her shoulder. "Wait!" he said.

Velmal's face was contorted with rage as he lifted a knife and grabbed Rotu around the chest. "Did you really believe I'd let this wedding go ahead?" he cried, holding the knife to the prince's throat. "Did you really think I'd let you all live happily ever after? Well, I'm not defeated yet!"

"I'm afraid that's where you're wrong, Velmal," Tom said. Velmal turned towards him. As their eyes met, the Wizard's thin lips twitched into an ice-cold smile. He pressed his knife closer to Rotu's throat, making the prince gasp with pain.

"I think not," Velmal said.

Tom smiled, and lifted his hand.

A loud crack rang through the tent. Velmal's face turned pale and his eyes went wide with panic. He let go of the prince, pushing him aside as he scrambled away from the sound. A bull's skull on the end of a bone-link whip was lashing towards the Wizard. It wrapped around Velmal's

ankle, then snapped back, tugging
the villain out through an open flap
in the side of the tent.

Through the gap, Tom could just
make out the lumpy green skin of
Grashkor the Beast Guard's huge leg.

"Aargh! No! Help!" Velmal's

terrified cries cut off with a strangled yelp. The flap of the tent fell shut.

Tom returned to his place beside Elenna and grinned at her astonished expression.

"That's why we're out here," Tom said. "So Grashkor could sneak up outside the tent – he couldn't have entered the city now that it's protected by the Treasures again. We knew Velmal would come back."

"So the Evil Wizard is on his way back to the Chamber of Pain?" Elenna asked.

"That's right," Daltec said. He turned to Aduro, who stood at his side. "I promise, I will be keeping a special watch on the prison island from now on."

A loud fanfare suddenly blared at the back of the tent, and the entrance at the front opened to reveal King Hugo. He was wearing a richly embroidered red gown, trimmed with gold, and grinning broadly. But as he looked inside the tent, his smile faltered. He put up his hand, and the fanfare came to a halt.

"Has something happened?" he asked, suddenly looking panicked. His eyes darted over the stunned faces of the guests in the tent. "Please tell me nothing has happened to the queen!"

Tom stepped forward. "Nothing has happened that you need to worry about, Your Majesty," he said. "Queen

Aroha will be arriving shortly."

The king let out a long breath, then drew himself up tall, the colour returning to his cheeks. "Thank goodness for that," he said. "I have been waiting for this day far too long. You know, Tom – I actually met Aroha when I was no older than you and Elenna are now. I knew even then we were destined for each other." The king winked meaningfully at Tom. Then he signalled to the musicians at the back of the tent.

The fanfare started up once more, and Queen Aroha entered the tent. She walked slowly, purposefully, in a wedding dress of crimson velvet, decorated with trails of diamonds sewn into the fabric. She was escorted by Epa and three of her ladies-in-waiting – all of whom held hefty broadswords in front of their faces, instead of bouquets.

Tom hurried back to his seat, his cheeks still burning.

Elenna glanced at him as he took

his place, then quickly looked down
at the floor. She'd clearly overheard
what King Hugo had said.

"Weddings do bring out the silliest
in people, don't they?" she said. "Who
wants to think about marriage when
there are Beasts to fight?"

Tom felt a rush of relief and
grinned at her. "Absolutely," he
said. "Beast Quests are far more
important than weddings!"

CONGRATULATIONS, YOU HAVE COMPLETED THIS QUEST!

At the end of each chapter you were awarded a special gold coin.
The QUEST in this book was worth an amazing 11 coins.

Look at the Beast Quest totem picture inside the back cover of this book to see how far you've come in your journey to become

MASTER OF THE BEASTS.

The more books you read, the more coins you will collect!

Do you want your own
Beast Quest Totem?

1. Cut out and collect the coin below
2. Go to the Beast Quest website
3. Download and print out your totem
4. Add your coin to the totem
www.beastquest.co.uk/totem

Have you read all the books in this series? Don't miss WARDOK THE SKY TERROR!

Read on for a sneak peek...

CHAPTER ONE

BANDITS

"There!" said Tom. "Do you see it?"

He pointed at the red mountain rising in the distance. Halfway up its slopes he could make out the city of Pania, built into the rock itself. A palace towered over the other buildings, made of the same red stone as the mountain. Flags fluttered from the turrets, and Tom could even see the glimmer of fires burning inside some of the halls.

Elenna jabbed him in the ribs.

"Don't be such a show-off," she teased. She was sitting behind him in the saddle. "You know no one else has a golden helmet to give us magical long-distance eyesight."

Tom blushed. "Sorry," he said. "Sometimes I forget!"

He wiped his brow and squeezed Storm's flanks with his boots. The poor horse seemed tired today, and no wonder – it had been three days'

hard riding from Avantia, along
with all King Hugo's retinue. To
make matters worse, this southern
realm of Tangala seemed to be
blessed with blazing sunshine all
day long. Even Elenna's wolf Silver
was panting as he trotted at their
side.

At least their journey was nearly
at an end. Tom couldn't wait to
reach Pania, the Tangalan capital,
and take a tour round the famous
city...

"Whoa, there!" said a familiar
voice at his side. Tom turned to see
the former wizard Aduro trotting
sideways as he fought to control his
mare. Somehow he'd got his hands
tangled in the reins.

"Need any help?" asked Tom, trying to keep a straight face.

"Certainly not!" said Aduro, as his horse stopped to nibble at the grass.

"Poor Aduro," whispered Tom to Elenna. "It's no wonder he can't ride very well. Back when he had magical powers, he never needed to learn!"

Read WARDOK THE SKY TERROR to find out more!

Discover the new Beast Quest mobile game from

MINICLIP
▶ PLAY GAMES

Available free on iOS and Android

  **amazon**.com

Guide Tom on his Quest to free the Good Beasts of
Avantia from Malvel's evil spells.

UNLOCK YOUR EXCLUSIVE
BEAST QUEST GAME
BATTLE SHIELD

DOWNLOAD THE APP TO BEGIN
THE ADVENTURE NOW!

* How to unlock your exclusive shield!

1. Visit www.beast-quest.com/mobilegamesecret

2. Type in the code 2511920

3. Follow the instructions on screen to
reveal your exclusive shield